For my mate Mouldy
M.R.

First published 2022 by Walker Books Ltd, 87 Vauxhall Walk, London SE11 5HJ • 10 9 8 7 6 5 4 3 2 1

Text © 2022 Michelle Robinson • Illustrations © 2022 Chris Mould

The right of Michelle Robinson and Chris Mould to be identified as author and illustrator respectively of this work has been asserted by them in accordance with the Copyright, Designs and Patents Act 1988

This book has been typeset in Zalderdash • Printed in China

British Library Cataloguing in Publication Data: a catalogue record for this book is available from the British Library

ISBN 978-1-4063-9594-5 • www.walker.co.uk

Isabelle
AND THE
CROOKS

Michelle Robinson

illustrated by

Chris Mould

WALKER BOOKS
AND SUBSIDIARIES

LONDON · BOSTON · SYDNEY · AUCKLAND

Isabelle Crook was an ordinary kid.

She lived in an ordinary street.

In an ordinary house.

With an ordinary family ...

of **CROOKS!**

Isabelle wasn't like the other Crooks.

She wasn't sneaky
like Daddy Crook

Stealthy
like Mummy Crook

Or cunning
like Grandma Crook

or Grandpa Crook.   And unlike Little Barney Crook, Isabelle

would never dream of breaking the law.

On Monday night, Isabelle Crook was brushing her teeth when Daddy Crook said, "Do you want to come out bank robbing, love? You'll like it – there'll be piles of money to count!"

"No, thank you," said Isabelle.
"I much prefer counting sheep."

On Tuesday night, Isabelle Crook was tucking her teddy into bed when Mummy Crook said, "I'm off to burgle the toy shop. Care to join me, darling?"

"No, thank you," Isabelle said firmly.
"Burglarising is AGAINST THE LAW."

On Wednesday night, Isabelle Crook was drinking her milk when Grandpa Crook said, "Lovely night for a spot of breaking—and—entering."

"Are you coming, Isabelle?" said Grandma Crook, "it's what good Crooks do."

"Not this Crook," said Isabelle.

On Thursday night, Isabelle Crook was reading a story when her parents popped their heads round the door.

"Fancy helping us plan the next job, dear?" said Daddy Crook.

"It's a big one," said Mummy Crook. "Super exciting!"

Isabelle put down her book. "Stealing things is NOT exciting," she said, "it is very, very naughty."

On Friday night, the Crooks were all set.

"We're going to steal the crown jewels!" said Grandma Crook.

"Are you coming, Isabelle?" asked Grandpa Crook.

"You always said you wanted to visit the tower," said Daddy Crook.

"Come on, Isabelle," said Mummy Crook, hot-wiring the family getaway car. "It'll take every last Crook to pull it off."

"LESS GO!" said Little Barney Crook, waving his crowbar.

Isabelle tutted. "Not you as well?"
She didn't even wave them goodbye.

On Saturday night, the Crooks went to bed early,

surrounded by the stolen crown jewels.

But Isabelle couldn't sleep.

The Queen must be very sad, she thought.

I'd be sad if someone took something precious to me.

So she grabbed a swag bag ...

gathered up the crown jewels ...

and tip-toed into the night.

She was sneaky.

She was stealthy.

She was cunning.

But as she went to put the jewels back on their pillow...

"Your Majesty," the police said,
"we've found the crook who took the crown jewels."

The Queen peered at Isabelle over the top
of her glasses.

"What do you have to say for yourself,
young lady?"

Isabelle didn't want her family to go to jail.
They might be crooks, but they were precious to her.
She'd be very sad if someone took them away.
So she took a deep breath and said, "I'm very sorry
about your missing jewels. Taking things that don't
belong to you is very naughty."

"She doesn't seem like a crook to me,"
the Queen said to the police.

But they still locked Isabelle in jail.

"Just for one night ...

to think about What You've Done."

On Sunday, the Crooks woke up to find everything GONE.
"Someone's stolen my swag bag!" said Daddy Crook.

"Someone's stolen my getaway car!" said Mummy Crook.

"Someone's stolen the crown jewels!"
gasped Grandpa Crook.

"Never mind all that," said Grandma Crook,
"someone's stolen Isabelle!"

"LESS GO!" said Little Barney Crook.

Isabelle sat in her cell listening
to the rain pit-patting
through the bars.

"At least the others aren't
in trouble," she said sadly.

"Psst!" said Daddy Crook.

"Care to join us, darling?" said Mummy Crook.

"Breaking out of jail is very naughty,"
said Isabelle, slipping through the bars.

"And very fun," said Grandpa Crook.

"You didn't deserve to be here anyway," said Grandma Crook.

"Not one bit," said Daddy Crook.

Mummy Crook kissed her.
"You're not an ordinary Crook."

But Isabelle wasn't so sure. She was already planning her next big job.

She snuck out on Monday night.

Tuesday night.

On Wednesday, Thursday and Friday.

Wherever Isabelle went,
her family went, too —
putting absolutely everything back
where it belonged.

They're sneaky!

They're stealthy!

They're cunning!

They're the Crooks!

And with Isabelle in charge,

they'd never dream of breaking the law...

Well, not often.